DRAGON CHILD

To the DragonTwins, Issy and Ellie

First published 2013 by A & C Black,
an imprint of Bloomsbury Publishing Plc
50 Bedford Square
London WC1B 3DP

www.bloomsbury.com

ISBN 978-1-4081-7625-2

A CIP catalogue for this book is available from the British Library.

Printed and Bound by CPI Group (UK) Ltd, Croydon CR0 4YY

1 3 5 7 9 10 8 6 4 2

MIX
Paper from
responsible sources
FSC® C020471

DRAGON CHILD

The Opal Quest

GILL VICKERY

Northern Sea

East Eldkeiler Mts

Fellhof

Drakelow Mts

Eastern Sea

Kulafoss

Drangur

Holmurholt

Askarlend

Roornhof

Southern Sea

The Story So Far...

Tulay was a peaceful land until a family of High Witches stole the DragonQueen's necklace, set with six jewels of power. The High Witches divided the jewels between themselves and used their power to drive the dragons away.

In revenge, a dragon took the youngest witch's daughter, Tia. Raised by dragons, Tia now wants to prove she is a true DragonChild by recovering the jewels and returning them to the DragonQueen. Her DragonBrother, Finn, is with her on the quest.

Tia and Finn first stole back the emerald, which grants the power to talk to animals, from the High Witch Malindra who ruled the town of Drangur. Now they are on their way to recover the opal, which grants the power to shapeshift. The jewel is kept by the High Witch Yordis in the town of Kulafoss.

Chapter One

The Mines of Kulafoss

Tia and Finn had been walking from Drangur for three days.

'Those valleys and mountains don't look any closer to me,' Tia grumbled, staring at the horizon where the hills rolled away in a blue haze. She was very tired after walking through endless grassland.

'They are, really,' her DragonBrother said. 'We should reach Kulafoss by nightfall.'

'We'd get there a lot quicker if I could ride you,' Tia said.

As she knew he would, Finn stopped in his tracks and glared at her.

'I'm a dragon, not a horse,' he said. 'I'll carry you in an emergency and that's all.'

Tia patted his soft hide. 'I know.' He'd rescued her when she'd fallen from the top of Drangur castle and flown her to safety. It hadn't been easy; he was only a small dragon, though strong.

Tia knew she shouldn't tease him. 'I'm sorry,' she said. 'I just need to rest a bit.'

They sat on the grass and Tia flopped against him. 'Tell me about Kulafoss.'

Finn had been there when he was very young, before all the dragons had fled to Drakelow to hide from the High Witches. 'At the end of a valley is a cliff and a *huge* waterfall plunges down it – it's the biggest in the whole island. The water comes from snow-melt off the Eldkeiler Mountains.' Finn sounded wistful: the mountains had been his home until the witches drove the dragons away.

'Where's the castle?' Tia asked.

'It's carved out of the rock half-way up the cliff-face. The waterfall is right next to it. The castle's ugly but *very* impressive.'

Tia jumped to her feet. 'Let's go – the quicker we start, the quicker we can see it.'

Finn puffed out a few smoke rings. 'I've been saying that for ages,' he objected.

'Come on then!' Tia strode ahead as if she'd never complained of being tired. Finn followed, smoke streaming from his nostrils.

By the time they arrived at the open end of the valley it was night. Moonlight shone on the river flowing down it, and on the grassy slopes scattered with rocks and scree. There were trees growing further down the valley, though it was hard to see them properly; it was very dark in there.

'Shall we stop here until it's light?' Tia asked.

Finn agreed but as they made their way towards the valley entrance Tia began to feel uneasy.

'I think the spell to keep dragons away will cover the whole valley. You ought to change yourself so the spell can't see you,' she told her DragonBrother.

Instantly his hide rippled with shadows that matched the darkness they had walked into. 'It'll be hard work to camouflage myself all night. Let's go above the valley and sleep there. If you think it's outside the spell boundary,' he added.

'That would make sense, wouldn't it?' she said. She didn't tell Finn that she could see, from the corner of her eye, a faint shimmer like a gossamer thread running round the rim of the valley. When she looked at it straight on, it disappeared. She didn't want to tell Finn because she feared he might tease her and say she could only 'see' the spell because she was a witch-brat: that was what the other dragonets had called her, and she was afraid it might be true.

They settled in a dry hollow a short distance from the edge of the valley and Tia leaned against Finn's warm hide.

She was dozing off when he sat up suddenly, and she slithered down with a bump as he pointed to the other side of the valley. 'What's that?'

Tia peered into the darkness and saw a line of wavery yellow lights.

Dragons had sharper eyes than humans and Finn soon saw what the lights were. 'They're lanterns – people are coming this way.'

As they got closer Tia could make out a group of women walking in a straggling file. She and Finn watched as the line came to a halt and the women held their lanterns up high. The lights illuminated a dark hole in the hillside framed by thick wooden beams. 'What's that?' Tia said.

'There are crystal mines here,' Finn said. 'I think that's the entrance to one.'

'Look, someone's coming out of it.'

There was a murmur of excitement from the group as the first miner emerged.

'It's a child!' Tia said.

More and more children stumbled out and were hugged by their mothers.

'They look very tired,' Finn said.

'It's not right!' Tia said. 'How can their parents allow it?'

'Perhaps the witch makes them do it with the power of the opal,' Finn said.

Tia thought about that as the filthy, exhausted children were collected and led away down the valley. She clenched her fists and vowed that she would not fail to steal the opal and set the children free.

A horrible grinding noise made her jump, and she looked across at the mine entrance. Rocks were sliding down the slope towards it.

One woman still waited there. 'Magnus!' she called. 'Where are you?'

A little boy appeared. He was so tired that he swayed and rested against the wooden frame. His mother ran forward to help but before she could reach him, a shower of rocks and boulders tumbled over the entrance with a horrible rumbling.

'Magnus!' the woman screamed. 'Magnus!'

The little boy was trapped inside the mine.

Chapter Two

The Rescue

The boy's mother pulled frantically at the rocks piled up in front of the mine entrance. The other women and children ran back to help her.

'We've got to do something!' Tia said to Finn.

Finn didn't argue. He grasped Tia in his claws, changed his skin to the colour of night and flew across to the other side of the valley. As they landed, Tia said, 'I'll go down and help. Wait here.'

She scrambled off along a path winding down the rocky hillside, her feet slithering on loose shale. She reached the mine and started to help pull away the smaller rocks. Everyone was too busy to ask who she was. Soon only one huge boulder was left, wedged up against the entrance.

'Magnus!' The little boy's mother beat her hands against the stone.

'Mama!' a tearful voice called faintly from inside.

A big, strong woman put her arm round Magnus's mother. 'Now, Solay,' she said, 'let's all push together and see if we can move this rock away.'

The women and children arranged themselves around the boulder and put their hands on it. 'Push!' Solay shouted. Everyone heaved at the rock but it wouldn't budge. They pushed and pushed until they were exhausted. It didn't move an inch.

They stopped and stood, panting. 'It's no good,' Solay sobbed.

Tia looked up to the top of the valley and could just make out Finn amongst the shadows. 'We can do it,' she said. 'Let's have one more try.'

Now the women and children looked at her curiously. 'Who are you?' Solay said.

'I'm Nadya. I'm a Trader. I got lost during a fog and I'm searching for my people.' Tia had used this story before. 'I saw what happened and came to help.'

'A little slip like you!' said the big woman who'd comforted Solay.

'Leave her be, Halla,' Solay said, choking back a sob. 'At least she tried to help.'

'I'm sure I felt the rock move, just a little bit,' Tia said. She smiled at Solay. 'Let's try again.'

Halla shook her head. 'It won't move.'

'We have to try,' Solay said and braced herself against the rock. One by one all the women and children joined her. Tia made sure she was last. As Solay shouted, 'Push!' Tia waved at Finn, in a gesture that meant, *Come and help.*

He glided down on silent wings, hovered and dug his claws into cracks in the stone. He pulled hard just as everyone pushed. The rock swayed to one side.

'Push again!' Tia shouted. They heaved, and Finn strained at the boulder tugging as hard as he could. He flapped his wings fast for balance and a whoosh of air swept over the group round the boulder. Some people looked up, startled, but then Solay shouted desperately, 'Push!' and the strange draft of wind was forgotten as shoulders and hands shoved at the stone. With a mighty effort Finn wrenched it away, and Magnus tumbled out into Solay's arms. Finn let go of the great rock and soared up to the top of the valley, out of Tia's sight.

Halla clapped Tia on the back, almost knocking her over. 'You were right, Trader girl – thanks to you, we got Magnus out.'

'It was working together,' Tia said. That was true, but only because Finn had been on their team.

'You're on your own then, while you look for your parents?' Halla said.

Tia nodded. She was tired, and hoped she wouldn't make a mistake if Halla started questioning her.

The big woman hugged her. 'Come back with me for a meal and a bed. You'll have to sleep with the animals but as you're a Trader you won't mind that.'

After Solay had thanked Tia, the exhausted women and children made their way back to the town of Kulafoss, trudging down a stony path halfway up the valley side.

As they went further into the valley and through the trees Tia heard a muffled roaring sound. 'What's that noise?' she asked Halla.

The woman laughed. 'Wait and see!'

One by one the women and children left the line to enter small houses built into the hillside. Soon only Halla and Tia were left. 'Not far now,' the woman said. They walked on and the roaring noise grew louder.

'Look.' Halla pointed towards a steep cliff forming the end of the valley.

Tia gasped in astonishment at a white sweep of waterfall thundering down the cliff into the foaming river below. A moonbow stretched from side to side in a shining silver arc. Tia stood rapt until clouds drifted over the moon and the moonbow faded.

'Come on, girl – I've not got all night,' Halla called. Tia hurried after her into a little house set amongst trees.

What was that noise?

Tia yawned and opened her eyes. A bright sunbeam shone into the tiny room. The noise that had woken her sounded like a rushing wind.

It's the waterfall, she thought and sat up.

'Mind your elbows!' a voice said.

'Sorry,' Tia apologised to the young goat she'd accidentally prodded.

The goat looked at her in astonishment. 'You understand me!' he said.

'Oh!' Tia's hand flew to the emerald she kept on a chain under her shirt. The magic jewel allowed her to speak to animals but she wanted to keep it a secret.

Another goat got to her feet. 'She's probably a witch like Halla,' she said.

'I'm not a witch,' Tia insisted. She hated the fact that her birth mother was one of the High Witches who'd stolen the DragonQueen's jewels of power.

'You must be,' the nanny goat said, 'or you wouldn't be able to talk to us.'

'Just a minor witch,' Tia mumbled reluctantly. Minor witches could only do simple magic like sparking fire or charming warts; they weren't dangerous, so no-one took any notice of them. If Tia pretended to be one, it would stop the goat wondering how she could talk to animals.

She brushed straw from her clothes and crossed to the window, carefully avoiding a curled-up little sheep and the mice scurrying from under her feet.

She leaned out of the window and the thundering of the waterfall sounded even louder. Halla's house overlooked it, and in the bright morning sun a rainbow arched across the misty river and hundreds of tiny droplets shimmered in the spray.

But though it was beautiful, Tia was more interested in the grim and forbidding castle carved from the rocky cliff.

She shivered and looked away, towards the big stone houses, shops, inns and other buildings rising up on either side of the river. Above them, built into the hillside, were smaller houses like

Halla's, all linked by stony paths. Trees grew up the hillside wherever there was space. Not many people were about, just a few who were opening up their shops.

Halla poked her head through the curtains dividing the living rooms from the beast fold. 'Come and have breakfast,' she said.

Tia had been too tired to eat much the night before and felt empty. 'I'm coming!' she said and rubbed her stomach as it rumbled loudly.

Chapter Three

The Crystal Shaper

'My, you have a good appetite!' Halla said as Tia pushed away her empty plate.

'I'm always hungry,' Tia said. 'Can I do some jobs for you, to repay you for the food and bed?'

'I do need more fuel gathering for the fires,' Halla told her. 'But wait until the men and children have left for the mines.'

'Why do children work in the mines? And where do the men work? I didn't see any last night.'

'The men work in newer mines where the crystal is easy to get at,' Halla said. 'The children are used in the old mines where you can only find crystal that's hard to reach and it's an advantage to be small.'

'But it's so cruel!' Tia's life with the dragons had been hard and lonely but she'd never been forced to labour.

Halla nodded. 'It is. And we don't want to allow it but there's nothing we can do. The High Witch Yordis uses the DragonQueen's opal to force us to obey her.'

'How?'

Before Halla could tell her there was a knock at the door and she went to let in Solay and Magnus.

'Magnus was too tired to speak to you last night but he insisted on coming this morning to thank you,' Solay said with a big smile.

The little boy looked at Tia shyly and said, 'Thank you for helping Mama to roll away the rock. I was very scared in the mine.' His eyes filled with tears and he turned to his mother. 'Mama, do I have to go back?'

'Yes, but I'll make sure to be early and come inside the mine to fetch you. That won't be as scary, will it?'

Magnus shook his head.

Solay picked Magnus up and hugged him. 'That's my brave boy.' Tia could see that Solay's own eyes were shiny with tears. What could the witch Yordis do with the opal that frightened people so much?

A low sound like lots of drums beating sounded from the stone streets running by the river. 'We have to go,' Solay said and hurried out with Magnus. The drumming noise grew louder and louder.

'What's that?' Tia asked.

Halla laughed grimly. 'The sound of people going to the mines.'

Tia ran to the door and looked out. Dozens of men and children, some with their mothers, were tramping in wooden-soled shoes towards the end of the valley.

'Aren't you going with them?' Tia asked Halla as they watched the workers trudge away, heads down, not talking.

She shook her head. 'I only went with Solay yesterday to keep her company – she's my sister.'

'What do you do?' Tia asked her, hoping Halla would tell her about being a hedge witch.

'I'm a washerwoman,' Halla said. 'That's why I need a lot of fuel for my tubs, to heat the water.'

Halla took Tia outside and showed her a crude sledge pulled by two straps. She gave her a large ball of leather strips.

'When you've loaded wood onto the sledge, tie it down with these. Now, off you go and fetch me as much timber as you can.'

The sledge wasn't too heavy and Tia pulled it along the pathway and up into the trees quite easily. But instead of starting to collect wood she left the sledge and went back to the town to look round.

Now the miners had gone the town was busier: servants in the grand houses hung bedding out of windows to air and others scrubbed away at stone doorsteps. Well-dressed people went in and out of the shops, chatting happily and buying all sorts of goods. The fine shops had wonderful things for sale: jewellery and beautiful clothes and more kinds of cheese and pastries than Tia had known existed.

The most fascinating places were the crystal-shapers' workshops. Their windows had displays of uncut crystal that looked like jagged stones encrusted with blue frost. Amongst them were shaped crystals of different sizes, from tiny to several inches across. All were rectangular and as clear as polished glass.

As Tia stared through one of the windows a man carefully placed a crystal, mounted like a little mirror on a gold stand, in the middle of the display. He smiled at Tia and beckoned her in. Curious, she went inside.

'Hello, Trader girl,' the man said cheerfully. 'I'm Hannes – what's your name?'

'Nadya,' Tia said.

'What are you doing on your own? I wasn't expecting your people to arrive just yet.'

Her heart beat fast in excitement. If Traders were arriving she might be able to see her friends Kizzy and Florian. She explained her story to the crystal shaper.

'Ah, you got lost on the grasslands – so you're a land Trader. We're expecting the Water Traders.'

Tia was disappointed that she wasn't going to see

her friends but still excited at the thought of meeting Water Traders for the first time; they travelled the rivers of Tulay and over great seas to other lands. 'When are they arriving?' she asked Hannes.

'In a few days, we hope; that's why we shapers are all busy displaying our best sunstones.'

'What are sunstones?'

'What do they teach you young people?' Hannes said. 'Water Traders and seafarers use them to find their way. Even in cloudy weather the sunstones gather hidden light and point sailors in the right direction. He reached towards the big crystal. 'Look.' He swivelled it so that the sun shone directly on it and brilliant beams of light instantly radiated from its core.

'Oh, it's beautiful!' Tia said.

The crystal shaper looked proud. 'This is my best one,' he said. 'I hope the Traders will give me a good price for it.'

Tia wondered if the price of little children working the dangerous mines was too high. She decided she'd seen enough of the beautiful crystals. She said goodbye to Hannes, went back to the sledge and pulled it all the way to the top of the valley.

Chapter Four

Yordis

Tia found Finn in the hollow, lying on his back and warming himself in the sunshine.

'I came as fast as I could,' she said. She explained about Halla, Yordis and the miners. 'You were so brave, helping to free Magnus,' she added. 'It must've been very hard to keep yourself safe from the spell *and* lift the boulder.'

'Yes, it was, though it's easier to disguise myself now I've practised,' he said.

Tia patted his snout. 'Now we've just got to decide how to get that opal back and save all the children from the mines! What do you think the High Witch does to frighten people so much?'

'The opal lets her change into whatever she wants. Perhaps she becomes a monster?' he guessed. 'A really horrible one.'

Tia shuddered. 'She must keep the opal in the castle. I'll have to get in there somehow.'

'Be careful,' Finn said anxiously.

'I will.' Tia jumped up. 'I have to go – I'll come back as soon as I know more.' She waved goodbye and went back to Halla's sledge. She worked fast and collected a big pile of branches. She knew how to tie strong knots and soon had the wood fastened down. She pushed the ball of leather strips into her pocket and sat on the edge of the sledge to have a rest before she started hauling it back to Halla.

A voice squawking above her head nearly made her jump out of her skin. 'Run! Run as fast as you can!'

A jackdaw perched on a branch above her head, flapping his wings furiously to get her attention. It was the bird who'd helped her defeat the High Witch Malindra and steal the emerald.

'Loki! You've come back!'

'Never mind that – run! A bear is coming!'

At that moment Tia heard a great crashing sound, and the ground juddered as though something huge was tramping swiftly through the trees towards her. She leapt up and ran as fast as she could, jumping over fallen logs, scudding down paths, and all the time she could hear the dreadful thundering steps behind her getting closer and closer. Something caught at her jacket and jerked her off her feet. She landed on her back with all the breath knocked out of her. She was too terrified to do anything but lie still with her eyes tightly shut.

'What have we here?' said a harsh, deep voice. 'A little Trader girl. I wonder what she'd taste like.'

Quaking with fear Tia opened her eyes. Rearing over her on its hind legs was a huge brown bear. It dropped onto all fours, poked its head close to Tia's face and sniffed.

As it reached forward Tia saw a collar around its neck, almost hidden by fur, and in the middle shone a milky-white opal glittering with shifting flecks of every colour.

This was Yordis, High Witch of Kulafoss! She'd used the power of the opal to turn herself into a monstrous bear.

Although Tia was terribly afraid of the gigantic animal looming over her, a plan quickly formed in her mind. Because the bear was really Yordis, it would be able to understand human speech, but it wouldn't know that Tia understood animal language. So, as it drooled on her jacket, Tia said, 'If I'm going to be eaten I'm glad it's by the most magnificent bear on Tulay.'

The bear blinked and cocked its head to one side. Tia tried to sound mesmerized with wonder as she said, 'My people have told me stories of the great Skrimsli Bear but no one said how majestic and... and... beautiful you are.'

She didn't really think the bear was beautiful: its breath smelt terrible, its teeth were dirty and its fur was mangy.

It sat down with an undignified thump and mused, 'This morsel of Trader child amuses me – I may spare it.'

Tia risked standing up. 'Not so fast,' the bear said, planting a massive paw on her shoulder and forcing her down.

Tia dropped to her knees and muttered, 'I hope I haven't offended the great Skrimsli Bear somehow, as Prince Kaspar did in the old story.'

The bear scratched its rump. 'I like stories.'

That gave Tia a lead. She said sadly, 'I wish I could do what Prince Kaspar did and tell tales to this wonderful creature. It would be such an honour. What a pity she can't understand me.'

'I want to hear these tales,' the bear snuffled. She stood up and waved a paw. 'Oh, get up – you grovel like a grooming maid.'

Tia pretended to be astonished. 'I think the Skrimsli Bear wants me to stand in her presence!' She got to her feet and bowed. 'O great and mighty one, it is an honour even to be in your shadow.'

The bear grunted, turned and lumbered off, the thud of its huge flat feet echoing through the trees. When the sound had died away Tia's legs folded and she slid to the ground.

Loki flew down.

'I'm not sure what you just did, but it was very clever,' he said.

'That was the High Witch Yordis,' Tia said.

'I thought it might be.'

'Then why didn't you help me? She was going to eat me!'

'I'm a bird – what could I do against a bear? Besides, there was no point in our both being eaten.'

Tia couldn't argue with that. 'I haven't got time to go back and tell Finn about Yordis. Will you take a message to him for me?' she asked the jackdaw. 'You'll have to come back to town with me first.'

Loki agreed and Tia wearily fetched the sledge and began to haul it back to Halla.

Halla was annoyed with Tia. 'What took you so long?' she demanded.

Tia told her about being chased by the bear. Halla gave her a big hug. 'You were very brave – and lucky! Here, sit down and eat while I get on with my work.'

Tia munched her way through bread and cheese while Halla stacked the wood under huge cauldrons of water and snapped her fingers to spark fire. While she waited for the water to heat up, she sat and made Tia tell her about the bear again. Tia described how the bear had caught her and then let her go.

'I think the bear might have been the High Witch,' she said cautiously. 'It wore a collar with an opal in it. Do you think it might be one of the DragonQueen's jewels of power?'

Halla nodded reluctantly. 'If the Lady Yordis is interested in you, it's best you get away from here as fast as you can.'

That wasn't what Tia had planned at all! 'Can't I stay another night?' she asked, trying to sound tragic. 'I'm so tired.' She yawned.

'All right, you can help with the washing today – that'll keep you out of sight – and be off tomorrow in case Yordis's guards do a sweep of the town.'

'Why do they do that?'

'To collect people to work in the mines, or worse, in the castle.'

Tia wondered how working in the castle could be worse than in the dangerous crystal mines but Halla had spoken so grimly she didn't dare ask.

Chapter Five

Into Kulafoss Castle

When Tia had finished helping Halla she went to the stable room, exhausted from hauling hot washing in and out of the big tubs. Loki was waiting for her on the window ledge.

'Have you done that message you want me to take to Finn?'

'Not yet.'

She rummaged in her bag for her silver-tipped pen and wrote in her green book. She tore the page out, folded it small and knotted it to Loki's leg with a piece of leather strip.

'Finn's on top of the valley side,' she told the jackdaw. 'He'll be glad to see you.'

'We won't be able to talk,' Loki grumbled. 'You know dragons and birds don't understand each other.'

'Never mind, I'll come and talk to both of you when I can.'

Loki fluffed his feathers in annoyance then dived neatly out of the window and soared up into the sky. Tia flopped on the straw and was deeply asleep in no time. She didn't even stir when Halla brought in the animals.

After breakfast next morning Halla sent Tia on her way.

'Go to the end of the valley,' the woman said, 'and follow the river. After several days you'll reach safety.'

'Thank you,' Tia said and set off. She waited until the washerwoman went back inside her house then scrambled up into the trees and doubled back towards the waterfall.

She looked up past the booming wall of water and wondered how she was going to get into the castle; there weren't any steps or ramps leading up to it. The only link between the gate and the ground was a large metal tube made out of criss-crossed bars of iron. There was an open archway at the bottom.

Tia didn't see how the tube could help her get into the castle – she certainly wasn't going to climb up it!

She wandered nearer to the waterfall in case there was a way in behind it. Close to, the water thundered so loudly she didn't hear the metal tube begin to rattle and clank as a rickety cage cranked down it.

She came to a little hut tucked away in a cleft of the rock. She looked inside but it was empty except for what seemed to be a very large, curled-up flag in one corner.

She followed a narrow, rocky path that led behind the waterfall but as a dense, freezing mist sprayed over it she decided not to explore any further until she could find something to cover her clothes so they didn't get soaked. She turned, and took a step backwards in fright as she came face to face with four men in uniform.

'Look at this, lads,' one said as he grabbed Tia's arm. 'Our little bird's flown *into* the trap – this is going to be the quickest sweep I've ever done!'

'Sweep' – these men must be the guards that Halla had told her about.

The man pushed Tia inside the cage. 'You carry on with the rest of the sweep,' he told the other guards, 'and I'll take our sparrow here to the Lady Yordis.'

He pulled a handle and the cage began to jerk its way upwards on a cable, swinging and banging on its way. 'Hope you're not going to be sick,' he said, grinning.

Tia couldn't speak for terror as the ground dropped away under her and the cage lurched up to the castle entrance. There was nothing between her and the ground except for a lattice of bars! She was so frightened that when they reached the castle entrance she felt as though her legs had turned to water: the guard had to support her as he marched her out.

Kulafoss castle was grimmer than Drangur, and so dark Tia found it hard to memorise where the guard was taking her as they sped through winding corridors.

Eventually he stopped outside a thick wooden door and banged on it.

'Oi! I've got the Trader girl – let me in.'

The door swung open and the guard pushed Tia forward.

'She's all yours, Katinka. I'm off to report to the Lady Yordis,' he said to the girl inside and left.

Katinka was a few years older than Tia.

'You're very small,' she sniffed. 'And your clothes are ridiculous.'

Tia bristled. She thought her Trader clothes were very practical and she liked the bright colours.

Katinka went over to a cupboard and pulled out some clothes including a skirt, a top and a jacket, all in a faded pink. 'You can have these. Give me yours and I'll take them to the laundry.' She sniffed again. 'You smell like you've been sleeping among animals!'

Tia glared at the girl but obediently went behind a screen and threw her clothes over it to Katinka.

'There's hot water in the basin by the fire. Get washing while I go to the laundry.'

Tia scrubbed away using the same kind of Traders' soap as she had in Drakelow where she lived with her DragonMother, Freya. Tears came into her eyes as she felt a pang of homesickness. But there was no time to feel sorry for herself. She plunged her head into the water and rubbed hard at her gritty hair.

By the time Katinka came back Tia was washed and her hair stood up in damp, red-gold spikes. But she'd rummaged in the cupboard and found clothes she liked better than those Katinka had given her.

'You can't dress like that! You look like a boy!' Katinka said.

Tia looked down at the grey tunic and trousers she'd swapped for the pink garments. 'I don't care,

I'm not wearing that horrible long skirt – I keep treading on it and falling over.'

Katinka pushed Tia outside and along yet more corridors till they came to grand door with a carved surround. The girl knocked timidly.

A loud roar came from inside. Tia knew it was the bear saying, 'Enter.' So Yordis was still in her animal form! Tia would have to pretend to be surprised at not seeing a human. Hesitantly Katinka, who'd only heard the roar and wasn't sure what it meant, opened the door. She led Tia through a central chamber into a bedroom where she curtsied to the bear slumped in front of a fire.

Tia gave a gasp of astonishment and bowed extravagantly. 'I didn't expect to see you, O great Skrimsli Bear!'

The bear ignored her and grunted at Katinka, who ran towards a table and hurriedly picked up a tray of brushes.

'The High Witch Yordis wishes me to teach you how to be a grooming maid.' She rolled up her sleeves and Tia saw lots of bruises. *Yordis must've done that – no wonder Katinka's afraid of her*, Tia thought, and felt sorry for the girl. She felt even sorrier for her when the bear batted at her several times for snagging brushes in her fur.

'Now you try.' Katinka handed a brush to Tia. *Good luck*, she mouthed silently.

Tia was used to grooming the Traders' shaggy little horses with their long manes and tails and had no difficulty with the bear's fur. Yordis waved Katinka away and turned over with a snort. Tia wanted to laugh as she went on grooming. This bear with its dirty, tangled fur was her aunt! What would she think if she knew that her niece, a DragonChild from Drakelow, was picking burrs and fleas from her coat?

The bear's eyes closed and she began to snore. Tia grew bolder and brushed nearer and nearer to the collar; she wanted to have a close look at the magic opal.

All of a sudden the bear rolled over and pinned Tia to the floor with her huge paw. 'Do not touch my collar, Trader brat,' she snarled.

Tia could hardly breathe with the paw pressing into her chest. 'I've done something wrong,' she wheezed, trembling as growls rumbled deep inside the bear. 'I'm sorry. Perhaps you don't like to be groomed near to your collar?'

The growling increased.

'I'll be careful not to do it again, O great one,' Tia said quickly.

The bear lifted her paw. 'This girl's quick to work out what I mean. She keeps her wits about her and she grooms well. I'll keep her.' She flopped down again.

Tia sat up and gulped in air. Yordis wasn't very bright but she was dangerous and cruel. Tia was going to have to be very, very careful.

Chapter Six

Chimneys

When Tia had finished grooming the bear, she was taken for a meal in the castle kitchen. After that, Katinka showed Tia to a small room next to Yordis's chambers. It had two tiny, sealed windows. An unlit fire set was set into one wall and a little alcove next to it had a washing area. There was just enough space for a bed and a wooden chest where Tia stowed her bag.

Katinka told her, 'The High Witch says you have to stay here till tomorrow, then she wants you to tell her some story about a prince and a bear.'

Tia had forgotten about that! She sat on the bed, hoping Katinka liked to gossip.

'Yordis can't always be a bear. I mean, she must be a human being sometimes, otherwise she couldn't tell you what she wants.'

'The *Lady* Yordis chooses when to be herself. At those times she usually stays in her room.'

'Why?'

'You ask too many questions,' Katinka snapped, and Tia decided not to ask where the High Witch kept the collar when she wasn't wearing it.

'I'll bring you some food later,' Katinka said, and left.

Tia got out her book and pen and scribbled down a map of the parts of the castle she remembered. She'd add to it as she learned more. Then she thought about the story she was going to tell Yordis next day.

Much later, the door opened and Katinka came in with a tray of cold left-over food and drink. Tia hoped she'd stay to chat but the girl only said, 'I'll come for you in the morning and take you to the High Witch,' then went away.

Tia poked her fork into some cold meat. She was stuck in a room with windows Loki couldn't fly through; how was she going to get a message to Finn?

She shivered. It was growing dark and the room was so cold! She hurried to the fireplace and found a box with moss and flints inside. She pushed the moss among the sticks and fire-rock in the hearth and struck the flints together, but the moss was slightly damp and the sparks wouldn't catch.

'I wish I *was* a hedge witch!' Tia grumbled, snapping her fingers as Halla had done to ignite the sticks under her cauldrons of water.

Whoosh! Fire ate up moss and sticks, turned the black fire-rock to glowing red, and roared up the chimney, scattering handfuls of sparks like little red sprites.

Tia fell back in shock. No hedge witch could have conjured up fire like this. Tears stung her eyes. The dragonets had been right after all: she was a witch-brat.

She sat for a long time, turning over and over in her mind what to do. Eventually she decided to keep her new-found ability a secret: she wouldn't even tell Finn, and definitely not Loki. No-one was going to compare her to her evil aunts, the High Witches of Tulay.

The fire had begun to die down. Cautiously Tia added more fire-rock and blew gently to fan the flames. To her relief they flickered and danced quite normally. She'd just have to be very careful not to let this unexpected magic ability show.

She yawned and stumbled into bed and instantly fell asleep

Katinka woke her the next morning. 'I see you found the flints,' she said nodding towards the embers in the hearth. She put Tia's freshly laundered Trader clothes on the chest. On top of the clothes was a small tray with a mean breakfast. 'Hurry up and get ready. The High Witch wants her story.'

Tia looked gloomily at the bread and cheese on the tray; it wasn't going to take her very long to eat that!

Yordis was in her own form, sitting in bed, lolling against heaped-up pillows with a large plate of food on her lap. Tia could see the High Witch was very like her sister, Malindra, but much broader and not so beautiful. She wasn't wearing the opal.

'Sit on the bed, Trader girl, and tell me the story of Prince Kaspar and the Great Bear,' Yordis said.

Tia obediently climbed onto the enormous bed and sat cross-legged. Katinka curtseyed. 'Is there anything more, Lady Yordis?'

'Who asked you to speak?' Yordis threw a chicken leg at the girl, who scurried out, glaring at Tia.

It's not my fault if Yordis likes stories, Tia thought.

'Now, girl, begin – and make it a good tale,' Yordis
ordered.

Tia told her made-up story. She acted out the
voices and made big gestures as she described Prince
Kaspar's fights. The further she got into the story
the more she liked it; she added details as she went
along and time flew by.

Suddenly Yordis screeched, 'Vermin!' She reared up and flung her plate at a little mouse scampering by the wall. Tia nearly fell off the bed with shock as the plate smashed into pieces and the mouse disappeared through a crack in the wall. Yordis, pale and trembling, sank back into her pillows.

'Mice!' she shuddered. 'I hate them!'

Tia bit her lip to stop herself from laughing out loud. Yordis, the mighty High Witch of Kulafoss who stalked her lands as a great and fearsome bear, was afraid of a tiny little mouse!

'I've heard enough for now!' Yordis said. 'We will continue the story tomorrow. Go to your room – and stay there.'

Tia did as she was told. She sat on her bed and wrote down more ideas for her story of Prince Kaspar. After a while she heard snuffling outside her room; Yordis was a bear again and checking on Tia. *She can't have gone far to change back so quickly,* Tia thought. *Perhaps the opal's in her chambers somewhere.* The snuffling stopped and she heard the heavy flump, flump, flump as the bear stamped away down the corridor.

Tia opened her door carefully and peered out. There was no sign of the bear.

Chapter Seven

The Secret Passage

For the next few days Tia continued telling Prince Kaspar's story to Yordis, who didn't seem to mind that the tale had no ending. She was never left alone in the witch's rooms and when she wasn't storytelling or grooming the bear, Katinka kept a close eye on her.

At night Tia explored and mapped the castle. She got to know its tower rooms, its cellars, its hall, kitchen and workrooms. She explored the weaponry and practised swinging heavy swords and lifting spears. She decided she preferred the sling she kept in her pocket: it was lighter and easy to hide.

By the time she finished her map she could find her way around the castle without any difficulty.

In the daytime, when she wasn't busy with Yordis, she chatted to the other servants and the guards in the big kitchen where they gathered in their spare time.

Two things puzzled Tia: firstly, how did the bear come and go from the castle? It was far too enormous to use the cage lift. Even in her human form it would've been difficult to fit Yordis *and* her bodyguard into it. Yet she somehow managed to enter and leave the castle without anyone seeing her.

The second puzzle was where Yordis kept the collar. Tia quickly learned people didn't like talking about it. One afternoon, when she spoke to the chief guard, he looked around furtively then answered in a low voice, 'You ask too many questions about things that don't concern you. It'll get back to the Lady Yordis if you're not careful, and she won't be happy to know you're interested in the opal. She keeps it hidden – even I don't know where it is.'

Though he was fierce, it was clear he meant well.

'Thank you,' Tia said. 'I was just curious but I won't mention it again.'

The guard patted her shoulder. 'You remind me of my little girl, Laufey. She's about your age. I don't see her so much now she's down the crystal mines.'

He sounded very sad.

'Why do you let her work there?' Tia blurted out.

'The Lady Yordis wished it – and if I had refused

she would've... done something very terrible. As she will to you if you continue to ask questions. Now, I see Katinka wants you.'

The maid had just finished filling a pail with corn and scraps; she pushed it at Tia. 'I'm too busy to feed the hens – you do it.'

Tia's heart beat a bit faster. The hens were outside in the courtyard; she might see Loki there. She took the pail and sauntered off, trying not to look too eager. 'Stay in sight!' Katinka warned her.

'All right,' Tia called back, though she didn't see how she could escape from the high-walled court-yard unless she grew wings.

The yard was busy with servants running about or gossiping and guards practising sword-fighting. The hen coop was open and the chickens were scattered about, rooting for food. Tia scanned the towers and the walls. There was a bird perched on top of a flagpole, looking down into the courtyard. She was almost sure it was Loki.

She rattled the pail and called loudly, 'Here chickens – food!'

At the sound of her voice the bird turned in her direction and the hens surged towards her, squab-bling and gurgling, with the cockerel scolding them to behave.

The bird flew down and perched on top of the roost. 'Hens are stupid creatures,' he said scornfully. It *was* Loki.

Tia scattered the feed as far away as she could and when the hens ran after it she slipped behind the wooden coop; the fowls wouldn't hear her and Loki talking there.

'I've been hanging around this castle for a week,' Loki complained. 'You disappeared from the wash-erwoman's, and there was no sign of you in the town, so I decided the witch had got you.'

'You're very clever,' Tia said, and smiled as Loki puffed up with pride. 'I knew you'd find me somehow.'

She reached into her jacket and pulled out a little wad wrapped with a leather strip from the ball she'd forgotten to give back to Halla. 'I've done another message for Finn.'

Loki sighed and stretched out a leg. Hastily Tia knotted the packet to it. 'I've written that the Water Traders will be here any day now. Yordis is herself when she trades. I'm going to try and find the opal then and steal it while she's busy.'

Loki liked shiny things. 'Where is it?' he asked eagerly.

'I don't know yet – but I'll find it,' Tia said firmly.

'Nadya! Nadya!' Katinka was in the courtyard searching for Tia.

'I've got to go.' Tia squeezed out from behind the roost; from the corner of her eye she saw Loki soar away into the sky. She ran up to Katinka. 'I thought a hen was stuck behind the coop,' she said.

'Lady Yordis is asking for you,' Katinka said. 'Hurry up.' Fear of the High Witch made her speak sharply.

'She won't eat you if I'm a bit late!' Tia said.

'She might.'

Tia started to laugh then realised Katinka meant what she'd said. As they hurried to Yordis's chambers Katinka told Tia that before Yordis took the opal she had been harsh but fair. 'And she was beautiful, too. But now she's spent so much time as the bear she's turning into a monster – ugly, greedy and cruel.'

Tia shivered as she remembered how the bear had caught her in the forest and towered over her, its fangs dripping, its fearsome claws gripping her tightly. The very thought of being eaten was enough to make anyone obey Yordis.

Tia made a decision: she was going to search Yordis's rooms for the opal as soon as she could. So, when the High Witch had heard enough of Prince Kaspar's adventures Tia returned to her room and waited.

When she thought enough time had passed she went to Yordis's chambers and knocked on the door. There was no answer. Carefully she turned the handle and peeked inside. All was still and silent; Yordis had definitely gone.

Tia explored each room including the ones she hadn't been into before - the bathing room and the library. There was no trace of the collar. She searched again, more urgently. This time she noticed that a big tapestry, stretching from floor to ceiling in the library, swayed a little as though a slight draft was blowing from behind it. When she looked there she saw a door. It creaked as she opened it. Behind the door was a dim passageway.

Tia stepped inside and pulled the door to. Instantly all was darkness.

Chapter Eight

The Crystal Cavern

Tia's hands touched rock on either side. She kept them against the walls as she stumbled forward a few steps. 'This is silly,' she said, her voice sounding very loud in the still darkness. She concentrated hard and then very, very gently clicked her fingers. To her relief one cold, little flame sparked into life and danced on the tip of her forefinger. She held it up like a candle and used it to illuminate the tunnel. It went down steeply, winding round and round, for a very long way. Gradually it levelled off and opened into a gigantic cavern.

Tia gazed in awe as crystal sparkled from the walls and roof. She carefully willed her little flame to grow brighter, and as it did, crystal lit up all over the cavern. It glittered from everywhere. There were even pieces scattered over the cavern floor like fallen

stars, so lovely that she picked some up and put them in her pocket.

She gazed around, sure Yordis's collar must be kept somewhere in the cavern. *But it's so big,* she thought. *It might take me for ever to find the right place!*

She searched and searched till her arm ached from holding the flame up to look into shadowy crevices, behind pinnacles and along ledges.

'Oh, this is hopeless,' she muttered and slumped against a cluster of pinnacles. She was too tired to concentrate on her flame and it dwindled to almost nothing. But as it dimmed another light began to fill the cavern.

Tia peered round the spikes of rock and saw a glowing ball of light drift into view, followed by the bear. Yordis had come back much sooner than Tia had expected!

She drew back a little but could still see the bear as it shambled to a stop in front of a sheer drop of crystal and shook itself. It shivered and blurred and Yordis appeared in its place. She unlatched the collar, reached high up and slid aside a panel of polished crystal. No wonder Tia hadn't noticed the hiding place: it was impossible to see in the sheet of crystal.

Yordis put the collar carefully into a space behind

the panel and slid it closed. Then she sighed and began to stretch and shake her limbs as if she had to get used to her human form again.

While Yordis was stretching, Tia tiptoed back to the tunnel entrance, pressing herself against the wall and slinking silently through the shadows. Just as she slipped inside to safety Yordis followed, the glowing ball lighting her way.

Tia ran as fast as she dared, burst into Yordis's library and closed the door quietly. She tiptoed to the central chamber door and was about to open it when someone knocked from the outside.

'Lady Yordis,' a voice said. It was Katinka! Tia was trapped between the High Witch and her maid!

She heard the door in the library bang shut, and Katinka knocked on the door again. She looked around wildly for a way out, and remembered the fireplace in Yordis's bedroom. It was wide; she could climb up inside it – if it wasn't yet lit.

She ran to it and saw with relief that it was swept and laid ready but not lit. She scrambled up the chimney. The rough bricks in the flu provided plenty of hand-holes and higher up there were some metal rungs to climb.

By the time Yordis returned to the bedroom Tia was out of sight. She heard Katinka knocking again and the bed creak as the High Witch threw herself onto it. 'Enter!' Yordis called.

There were the sounds of the door opening and closing and Katinka's voice saying, 'I've come to attend to the fire, Lady Yordis.'

Tia yelped in shock. She tried to stifle the sound with her hand and it came out as, 'Eeek!'

'There are mice in the chimney again!' Yordis said. 'Get that fire going, girl, and drive them away before I have to do it myself!'

Tia hastily scrabbled higher up the rungs. They passed a square hole, the entrance to a vent that she thought went in the direction of her room. She crawled inside it. There was no light so she snapped the tiny flame onto her finger again. The vent stretched away in front of her, narrow and thick with soot. She worked her way down it, levering herself along on her knees and one elbow so that she could hold out her flame with the other hand. It was hot in the tight passageway and a smell of smoke made her cough. She grimly crawled on.

A waft of air and a faint gleam of light told her she was near a flue. Surely it led to her room? She made the flame die away and crawled on as fast as she could. There was the flue! She eased herself into it and dropped into the cold hearth in her room.

Coughing and spluttering, she banged at her clothes. Soot puffed up in clouds. She scrubbed at her hair and more soot wafted out. How she was going to explain herself to Katinka?

Tia found Katinka in the kitchen. 'What have you been doing?' the maid exclaimed.

'I heard something in the chimney,' Tia said, 'and when I poked my head up to have a look, a load of soot fell on me.'

Katinka found the grey boys' clothes again and gave them to Tia. 'Have a good wash, change into these and bring me your Trader things to launder.' She sighed extravagantly.

Poor Katinka had to cope with Yordis and keep an eye on Tia. It was hard for her when Tia gave her extra work. 'I'm sorry,' Tia said.

'I know you don't mean to be a nuisance, you're a good girl really – most of the time.' Katinka smiled. 'I've heard that the Water Traders will definitely be here tomorrow so you'd better hope I can get these washed and dried tonight.'

'The Water Traders!' Tia danced up and down in excitement. *While Yordis is busy trading I can steal the opal!* she thought. Out loud she said, 'I wish I could see them.'

'I'll ask the Lady Yordis,' Katinka said. 'She gives us time off when the Traders are here, even the miners – so I think she'll do the same for you.'

That night, Tia sat on her bed and lined up the crystals she'd picked up off the cavern floor. She put the biggest in her bag and selected a smaller one that she tied a long strip of leather to. It was easy to tie the strip firmly to the crystal's jagged surface. When she'd finished she put it in a pocket in her bag, next to her sling and a small collection of smooth, round pebbles.

Now she was ready; tomorrow she would steal the opal.

Chapter Nine

The Water Traders

The lift was kept very busy next day as people left the castle, eager to meet and barter with the Water Traders. Tia was given permission to go down into the town too.

'Promise me you won't try and run away,' Katinka said.

'No, of course not – I don't want to get you in trouble with the Lady Yordis,' Tia said.

'Here.' Katinka gave her a mark. 'You work hard – you should have something to trade with.'

Tia thanked the maid and put the coin in her pocket. She felt guilty taking it from her because she'd soon have lots of marks of her own.

For once the town was busy: families with children filled the paved streets running along the riverside with its little stone-built quays and berths. The boats rode the river's current and the Traders skilfully skipped from the swaying decks to the riverside and back again as they laid out their wares.

Many of them greeted Tia as she hurried by in her bright, freshly-laundered Trader clothes. She longed to stop and talk to them but first she had to see Hannes, the crystal shaper.

'Why, it's Nadya!' he said with a smile. 'What are you doing here?'

'I've got a crystal to trade,' she said and showed him the largest of the ones she'd found on the cavern floor.

'This will make a fine sunstone,' Hannes said holding it up to the light and turning it this way and that. 'Where did you get it?'

'I found it.'

'Where?'

'That would be telling.'

Hannes stared at her for a moment then said, 'Traders are honest folk, so we'll leave it at that. I'll give you ten marks.'

'Twenty,' Tia said.

They bargained hard until they shook hands on

fourteen marks then Tia said goodbye and went back into the crowded street. Now she could buy what she needed.

She wandered through the cheerful crowds, trading for a new set of clothes which she rolled up tightly and put into her bag. Then she bought some candles and added those to her bag as well.

The Water Traders were friendly, and a woman invited her on deck to share a meal. As they sat and ate, Tia told her made-up story of losing her parents and asked if there was any news of the land Traders.

'We haven't seen our land cousins for some time,' the woman said. 'I heard they're going towards Stoplar. It's a bleak, harsh place but there's good trading to be had there for the land-bound.'

'I'll look for my parents in Stoplar then,' Tia said. 'But I'm staying here first, to listen to your story-telling and music.'

The woman smiled. 'We like to start in the evening when the hardest of the trading has finished.'

'Is that when the High Witch joins you?' Tia asked.

'She comes in the afternoon to trade in crystals, and feasts in the evening as we entertain her.'

'So she isn't here yet?'

The Trader shook her head. 'Not till the sun tells midday.'

Tia glanced up at the sun. It wouldn't be long now before Yordis was due to appear in the town; that would give Tia a chance to get into the witch's chambers and from there to the crystal cavern and the opal. She stood up and said, 'Thank you for the food,' to the Trader.

'You're very welcome. Good fortune in your search for your parents.'

'And good trading to you.'

Tia jumped from the boat to the street and ran in the direction of the castle but on her way she came face to face with Halla.

'What are you doing here?' the washerwoman said.

Tia tried to look small and vulnerable. 'I was caught by the guards and the Lady Yordis made me her grooming maid.'

'Why don't you run off now?' Halla said, standing firmly in front of Tia, her arms crossed.

Tia made her eyes round and sad. 'If I do that, she'll eat one of the other maids.'

'I see,' Halla said, more gently. 'Never mind, what's done is done. Let's make the most of the next few days while the Traders are here. Come with me – I'm on my way to join Solay and Magnus. They'll be pleased to see you.'

'I want to buy some sweet pies first,' Tia said.

Halla laughed and told Tia where to meet up later, and Tia pretended to go to a baker's shop. She didn't like lying to Halla but she had to get into the castle while Yordis wasn't there. Tia was determined to steal back the opal; after today, Yordis would never threaten the people of Kulafoss again.

When Tia reached the tube she found that the cage was up at the castle entrance. She would have to wait for it to come back down. No-one else was waiting but assembling by the little hut at the base of the waterfall were the chief guard and four men. They were setting down what looked like a bed supported on two poles that ran down its length.

I suppose the bodyguard is going to carry Yordis in that litter, Tia thought. *But where is she?*

She sneaked closer and hid under a mossy overhang of rock and watched as the guards raised a canopy over their heads and marched through the mist and spray and behind the waterfall. After a short while they marched back out again, this time with Yordis sheltered under the middle of the canopy. So this was how the High Witch came and went from the castle to the town! Tia could do that too – and go directly to the crystal cavern.

Once they were clear of the water the guards lowered the canopy and stowed it away in the little hut. Yordis lay down on the litter, the guards heaved it up and the chief guard marched them into town.

Tia waited till they disappeared from view then hurried to the hut. She covered herself in the canopy and followed the narrow, stony path behind the booming waterfall. It was so hard to see with the canopy covering her head that she almost missed a shallow entrance in the cliff. She stumbled inside and instantly the noise that had been pummelling her ears lessened. She dropped the heavy canopy in relief, snapped a flame onto her finger and gazed around.

Chapter Ten

The Opal

Some light filtered through the curtain of water but it wasn't enough to allow Tia to see clearly. She lit a flame on her finger and shadows loomed up the wall of a wide cave that sloped downwards as it went deeper into the cliff. Right at the back was the entrance to a tunnel.

I bet this leads to the crystal cavern! Tia thought.

She was right. After a long winding climb she found herself in the in the cavern standing in front of the smooth sheet of crystal that the collar was hidden behind.

'Now, where is that panel Yordis slid open?' she murmured.

She pictured the great bear standing on its hind legs and reaching out for the panel. She thought she knew roughly where it was.

Now she could put her plan into action.

She took the candles out of her bag, stood them in a circle round her and lit them with the flame on her finger. She snuffed her flame out; she needed both hands for the next part of her plan.

She picked up her sling and slotted a smooth pebble into the little leather cradle in the middle of the strings. She flicked the sling into the air, twirled it above her head then let go of one of the strings. The pebble flew out and hit the crystal sheet exactly where she thought the panel was; with a splintering sound, a pattern of cracks spread out like a spider's web.

She threw another pebble, and another. On the third attempt the panel shattered and splinters of crystal fell chiming to the ground. Now Tia could see the cavity that held the collar!

She couldn't help whooping with excitement, but she had no time to celebrate. Yordis was unpredictable: she might get bored with trading and come back at any moment to turn into the bear.

Tia took out the crystal she'd tied with leather strips the night before and placed it in the sling. She aimed carefully and slung the crystal into the cavity, hoping the strip would become entangled with the collar so that she could pull it towards her.

But the crystal only hit the collar and bounced back.

At that moment, an ear-splitting wail echoed around the cavern:

'*I'm being stolen! Rescue me! Thief! Thief!*'

Tia realised with shock that the collar was magically protected. Yordis must have put a spell on it so that it called out to her when it was in danger; wherever she was she would hear it.

It went on calling.

'*Thief! Rescue me! I'm being stolen!*'

Tia's hands were shaking – she was doomed if Yordis came back and caught her! And Katinka and others would suffer too. Desperately she tried again and again to entangle the collar but she was so frightened she kept missing. If only that collar would stop shrieking!

'Shut up!' she shouted at it.

It carried on screeching.

Concentrate! she told herself sternly. She ignored the bawling collar, took a deep breath, swung the sling round her head so fast it hummed, and let fly.

The stone shot to the back of the cavity; she pulled carefully, and felt it catch. She tweaked the leather strip – and the collar came tumbling down. As it hit the floor it stopped squawking, almost as if the breath had been knocked out of it.

A different screeching came from the tunnel.

'My opal! Who dares to steal my opal? I'll turn them into bear meat!'

Yordis was thundering towards the cavern, angry and ready for revenge.

Quickly Tia pushed the sling back in her bag and blew out the candles. The cavern was plunged into darkness.

She fumbled the collar over her head, pressed the opal against her neck and wondered what she could turn herself into.

It had to be something that would terrify Yordis; she was still a High Witch and even without the opal she was powerful and dangerous. Images flashed through her mind: a wolf, an eagle, a polecat?

Yordis, soaking wet and wild-eyed, burst into the cavern, her light-ball shining in front of her. It lit up Tia.

Yordis screamed until the crystal vibrated with the sound.

'A mouse!'

Whiskers twitching, Mouse-Tia advanced on the High Witch. Yordis screamed again and lumbered up the tunnel to the safety of her chambers.

Tia knew it wouldn't take Yordis long to work out
that the little mouse was really the opal thief. She
turned back into herself, snatched up her bag and
hared towards the cave. Just as she reached it a voice
shrieked, 'You!'

Yordis had used magic to skim fast above the
ground. She was catching up!

Tia dashed out of the cave, and burst from behind the waterfall – straight into the guards. A big crowd had followed them.

'What's going on?' the chief guard said, grabbing Tia's arm.

'The opal's been stolen! Yordis is really angry!'

The man's grip tightened. 'She's lost the opal? Are you sure?'

Tia nodded.

Yordis stormed into view. The chief guard let go of Tia's arm, and she immediately dashed into the crowd.

'Stop that child!' she heard Yordis shriek, and the chief guard answered, 'No.'

'Do as I say! Or…'

'Or what?' he snarled. 'You can't use your power on all of us, not now the opal has gone.' His eyes glittered in triumph. 'Let's get her, men!' he yelled. 'Think of our children!'

The crowd surged forwards chanting, 'Get her!' and 'Free our children!'

Tia knew that the guard was right: together, the people of Kulafoss were more than a match for Yordis.

The witch cowered as the guards took her by the arms and marched her away. Half the crowd

streamed after them and half ran towards the mines to rescue the children.

Tia hurried to a quiet place among the trees. She thought for a moment, wondering what animal to turn into, and imagined herself as an eagle.

The whole world became different! Her eyes were sharper, her hearing keener and she had an urge to soar into the sky. She grasped her bag with her talons, flapped her wings experimentally and then, without knowing how she did it, launched herself into the air. She was flying!

She balanced on the air for a moment, enjoying the sensation of floating high in the sky. *Why aren't I scared of heights now?* she wondered. She didn't know. She wheeled round and flapped her wings, pushing against the air, soaring and circling above the valley.

She soon spotted Finn stretched out on the grass and Loki perched on a rock nearby. She glided down, landed next to her friends and turned back into herself.

'You got the opal!' Finn said.

Tia laughed, took the collar off and showed her DragonBrother the jewel. Loki hopped up for a closer look, his eyes gleaming almost as brightly as the shimmering opal. Tia quickly put the collar back on.

'Now I can turn into a bird and fly, we can get to Stoplar much more quickly than by walking.'

Finn looked doubtful. 'It's a long way and you're not used to flying.'

Tia laughed. 'It's easy.' It was true: once she'd become an eagle, flying was simple. 'But if you like I can practise first.'

Before Finn could protest, Tia was an eagle again. She flew upwards – wheeling, stooping, hovering. How could she ever have been afraid of looking down on the world from high above the ground? Flying was glorious. *Maybe*, she thought, *I can turn into a dragon one day.*

She swished through the air. Yes, being a dragon would be wonderful! But first she had to fly to Stoplar and steal the topaz from the High Witch Luona.

Tia's adventure continues in

The Topaz Quest

published by A & C Black
February 2013

Tia's adventure begins in

The Emerald Quest

published by A & C Black

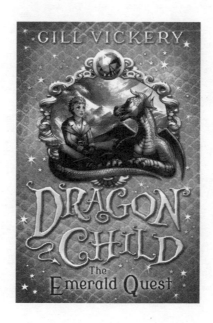